Sharks

Stan Cullimore

Illustrated by
Paul Savage

FULL FLIGHT

Titles in Full Flight Action

Web Cam Scam	Jillian Powell
Nervous	Tony Norman
Splitzaroni	Kathryn White
Missed Call	Jillian Powell
Space Pirates	David Orme
Basketball War	Jonny Zucker
Survival	Chris Buckton
Killer Sharks	Stan Cullimore
Sprinters	Jonny Zucker
Dangerous Stunts	Jonny Zucker

Badger Publishing Limited
Oldmedow Road, Hardwick Industrial Estate,
King's Lynn PE30 4JJ
Telephone: 01438 791037

www.badgerlearning.co.uk

Killer Sharks   ISBN 978 1 84424 245 0

First edition © 2004
This second edition © 2014

Text © Stan Cullimore 2004
Series editing © Jonny Zucker 2004
Complete work © Badger Publishing Limited 2004

Series Editor: Jonny Zucker
Publisher: David Jamieson
Editor: Paul Martin
Design: Jain Birchenough
Cover illustration: Paul Savage

4 6 8 10 9 7 5 3

Killer Sharks

Stan Cullimore

Illustrated by
Paul Savage

Contents

Chapter 1	The Dolphins	4
Chapter 2	Shark Attack	10
Chapter 3	Mr Gall	14
Chapter 4	Come and Get It	21
Chapter 5	Back in the Life Raft	26
Chapter 6	Friends in the Navy	30

Badger
L E A R N I N G

Chapter 1 - The Dolphins

Bob turned to his dad. "Can I steer the boat now?"

Dad shook his head. "Not yet. Your sister has still got five minutes left."

Bob looked at the three fishing rods hanging over the edge of the boat and groaned. "Fishing is boring."

"We haven't even started yet," Dad replied. "Anyway, how can you be bored? We're on a power boat. The sun's shining. We're in the middle of the deep blue sea, having a great holiday. You should be thrilled."

"He will be when he gets to steer the boat," muttered Hannah.

Bob scowled across at his little sister.

Dad moved his arm across Bob's wrist and pointed out to sea. "I think we'll stop over there."

"Great," said Bob.

"What's the time?" asked Dad.

Bob went to look at his watch. "Hey! My watch has gone!"

"Here it is." Dad grinned and held it up.

Bob reached for the watch and shook his head. "Give it back, Dad. And stop doing stupid magic tricks."

"It's not a magic trick," said Hannah. "He just took it without you seeing him." She put her arm round her dad. "You could have been a great pickpocket, Dad."

"Thanks," he grinned. "Having quick fingers can be very useful in my line of work."

Bob put his watch back on and looked at it. "Hey, it's my go now!"

Hannah let go of the wheel and Bob took over. He pushed a lever beside the wheel and the motor roared. The boat shot across the water.

"Now this is more like it," shouted Bob over the noise.

"Look!" cried Hannah. "Dolphins!"

Bob slowed the boat as three dolphins swam in front of it.

"Are they the sort you work with, Dad?" asked Hannah.

Dad shrugged.

"You know he can't talk about his work," Bob sighed. "He's David Brown, secret agent!"

"Not quite. But that's the trouble with working for the navy," Dad smiled. "Now if I was a pickpocket – I'd tell you all about my work!"

Suddenly the dolphins stopped playing beside the boat and dived out of sight.

"Where are they going?" cried Hannah. "I wanted to get out and swim with them."

"You're not going swimming out there," said Dad. "Look!"

He pointed at several large shark fins that were cutting across the water. They were heading right for the boat.

Chapter 2 - Shark Attack

The sharks circled the boat.

"Don't move," said Dad quietly. He opened a box in the bottom of the boat and pulled out a large orange bag.

"What's that?" asked Hannah.

"It's a life raft," Bob answered.

One of the sharks bumped against the boat. Hannah lost her balance and fell to the floor. Dad helped her up. "I don't like the look of this," he muttered.

Another of the sharks bumped the boat. There was a loud click.

Dad pulled a cord. The life raft began to inflate. A ticking sound came from under the boat.

"What are you doing, Dad?" asked Bob.

"Get in," Dad ordered. He pushed the life raft into the water. They all climbed in and Dad started rowing away from the boat as fast as he could.

"This is crazy!" shouted Bob. "What about the sharks?"

"I work with sharks," said Dad quietly. "These ones have been trained. I can tell."

"To do what?" asked Hannah.

"To carry mines. And to blow up boats!"

Suddenly the sharks all dived away from the boat. The ticking got louder.

"Heads down," shouted Dad. Seconds later, there was a loud explosion.

Hannah and Bob looked up just in time to see the boat sinking into the sea. A noise drew their gaze up as a helicopter flew into sight. It came closer and dropped a ladder towards the life raft.

Dad looked worried. "We might as well climb up it, kids. But I don't think I'm going to like what I see at the top."

Chapter 3 - Mr Gall

Once they got inside the helicopter,
Dad groaned.

"I thought it might be you, Gall."

The man he was talking to was short,
with long white hair. He threw back his
head and laughed.

"Mister Gall to you!" The man looked at Hannah and Bob. "So, Mr Brown. Are these your children?" he sneered.

Bob clenched his fists. "Yes, we are. What are you going to do about it?"

Mr Gall smiled. "Well, as long as your dad tells me what I want to know – nothing!" he shrugged. "But, if he won't talk, who knows?"

Dad put his arm around Bob and Hannah. "I'm not telling you anything, Gall."

Mr Gall reached into his pocket and pulled out a little box. It looked a bit like a mobile phone.

"Have you ever seen one of these, David?"

He nodded slowly. "You know I have. I invented them."

Bob and Hannah looked at their dad.

Mr Gall smiled at the two children. It was an evil smile. "This little box can be used to control those sharks down there," he said quietly. "With this clever little thing I can make them swim where I want them to. I can also make them attack whatever I want them to."

Bob and Hannah gasped and looked at their dad again.

Mr Gall put the little box back in his pocket. "Now children, I want your dad to help me invent a new box. One that has even greater range!"

Dad shook his head. "No way, Gall!"

Mr Gall sighed. "I thought you might say that."

Without any warning he turned and pushed Bob. The boy fell backwards out of the helicopter door with a cry.

Dad rushed forward and leant out. Bob was hanging from the ladder.

"You could have killed him!" shouted Dad.

Mr Gall pulled out a gun and grinned.

"What do you say now, David?"

Dad shook his head again sadly.

Mr Gall turned quickly and pushed Hannah out of the helicopter. Dad cried out. Mr Gall laughed and looked out of the window.

"Well, I can see the girl. She's in the life raft. But the boy is nowhere to be seen."

He laughed again. "Perhaps the sharks have got him already."

"No, they haven't!" cried Bob. He was climbing up the ladder. He was almost back in the helicopter.

"David, why don't you help your son?" Mr Gall sighed.

Dad pushed past Mr Gall, bumping against him as he went.

"Watch out, you clumsy fool," snarled the short man.

Dad leant out and grabbed Bob by the hand. At that moment, Mr Gall shoved him in the back.

"Aah," cried Dad as he and Bob fell head first out of the helicopter. They landed in the life raft next to Hannah.

She looked out and saw a row of fins getting nearer.

The sharks were moving in.

Chapter 4 - Come and Get It

"How are you getting on down there?" asked Mr Gall, leaning out of the helicopter.

"Get lost!" shouted Bob.

"It's OK," said Dad. "He can't harm us now!"

Mr Gall smiled. "Maybe I can't harm you. But my killer sharks can." He laughed. "I think it's time for them to attack you." He put his hand into his pocket. He frowned. He tried his other pocket, then frowned again.

"Looking for this?" asked Dad. He held up the little box that controlled the sharks.

"How did you get that?" shouted Mr Gall.

Dad grinned. "I picked your pocket."

"Well, aren't you the clever one?" Mr Gall sighed.

Hannah nodded. "Yes, he is!"

"No, he's not!" snapped Mr Gall. "He's just wasting my time." He waved his gun at Dad. "Give me the controller or else."

"Or else what?" shouted Bob.

Mr Gall grinned. "Or else, young man,
I'll shoot your sister!"

Dad groaned. "I might have known."
He held out the controller. "OK, Gall.
You win. Come and get it."

Mr Gall laughed. "I always win." He put his head back inside the helicopter and it began to move lower.

"Bob," said Dad quietly. "What's that thing you're holding?"

"I don't know," Bob replied. "It came off the float under the helicopter. I pulled it off by accident when I fell."

Dad looked at the big, flat plug Bob was holding. He frowned and looked up at the helicopter. Suddenly he burst out laughing.

"What's so funny?" asked Hannah.

"This is a plug," he grinned as he showed it to Hannah. "I can't wait until Mr Gall tries to land on the sea!"

"Why not?" asked Hannah.

"Because without this plug, water will get into the float under the helicopter. And when that happens..."

Bob burst out laughing. "The helicopter will turn over and sink!"

"Exactly," said Dad. They all turned to watch as the helicopter came in to land.

Chapter 5 - Back in the Life Raft

Once the helicopter was resting on the sea, Mr Gall appeared. He stood on the float and waved his gun slowly at Dad. "Now, the shark controller, if you please, David. And don't try anything."

Dad sighed. "What can I do from here?"

Mr Gall folded his arms.

Dad leant down and picked up a paddle that was lying in the bottom of the life raft. He dipped it into the sea and started to paddle towards the helicopter. Suddenly the paddle slipped from his hands.

"Dad, be careful!" gasped Hannah. Dad turned to her and winked. He looked down at the paddle and shrugged. Then he looked up at Mr Gall. "Now what do we do?"

"Get it out of the water, you fool," snarled Mr Gall. Dad smiled. He could see water pouring into the float. At that moment, the helicopter started to move. It rolled slowly over towards the life raft.

"Hey! What's going on?" cried Mr Gall as he lost his balance. He dropped his gun, which fell into the water and sank out of sight.

"The helicopter is sinking," said Dad calmly.

"Why?" cried Mr Gall.

Bob held up the plug. "I pulled this out of the float by accident. Sorry!"

"You stupid boy," screamed Mr Gall. By now, the helicopter was almost upside down. Mr Gall jumped into the water. "Move over you fools! I'm coming into that life raft."

Dad lent down. He quickly pulled the paddle out of the water.

"I don't think so," he said, and paddled the life raft away from Mr Gall. Then he pulled out the shark controller. "I think it's time to put the sharks to work." He grinned at Bob and Hannah. "Don't you?"

"Oh, yes," said Bob.

"Definitely!" agreed Hannah.

Chapter 6 - Friends in the Navy

"What's that noise?" asked Bob.

It was another helicopter.

"Perhaps they've come to help Mr Gall," said Hannah, looking worried.

Dad shook his head. He pointed to a green flashing light on the side of the life raft. "I don't think so. I set the radio beacon to send out a signal to my navy friends at work."

Sure enough, the helicopter was from the navy. The pilot leaned out of the window and waved at Dad. He turned and smiled at Bob and Hannah.

"It's OK. He's a friend of mine."

The pilot dropped a ladder down to the life raft. Dad, Bob and Hannah climbed into the helicopter and the pilot pulled the ladder up.

"What about Mr Gall?" asked Hannah.

"Are you going to leave him there?" asked Bob.

They all looked down. Mr Gall had climbed into the life raft. Dad looked thoughtful.

"No," he said. "I'm going to set the sharks on him."

"To eat him?" Hannah gasped.

Dad grinned. "No, just to tow him back to shore."

They all watched as the sharks closed in on the life raft.

"What's Mr Gall doing?" asked Bob.

"Why is he lying down like that?" added Hannah.

Dad smiled. "I think he's just fainted." He laughed. "He always was scared of sharks!"

***